# SILLY BIMBO VOLUME 1

## A BIMBO TRANSFORMATION ANTHOLOGY

### SADIE THATCHER

# INTRODUCTION

This is an anthology collection of multiple stories that are too short to publish as standalone books. But each story still has heart and a sexiness that I don't want to deny you, the reader.

Here's a little about each story.

- Two Bimbos was written for a writer's group contest, but I wanted an opportunity to share it more widely. Surprise! I won. Now you do too.
- Words Have Power was inspired by a suggestion another writer friend of mine made. I'm pretty sure you can figure out what the game is based on. I haven't played it, but it seems impossible not to know how the game is played after the social media firestorm it created.
- The Car Bimbo was written so that I could use the image on the cover. I've had it saved for a long time, wanting to find a good reason to use it. This story provided that reason.

# INTRODUCTION

- <u>Dealing With the Heat</u> was inspired by the mid-July, 2022 heat wave, both in Europe and locally where I live in the United States. The story is meant to take place in Europe, but I never actually specify that in the story. If you're reading this in Europe, you can pretend it takes place in the United States or Canada.

Thank you for reading this anthology book. There will likely be more that follow.

~ Sadie

# TWO BIMBOS

Candace Summers sat in the waiting room of the top cosmetic surgery practice in the world. Or at least that was what her research had told her. After coming into a bit of money, Candace had finally decided to correct what she viewed as her one flaw.

She had never been happy with her breasts. Candace was content or even happy with most aspects of her life, but her breasts, small, flabby, and asymmetric, always made her feel less than she had any right to feel. And so Candace had decided to get a breast augmentation.

The timing for all of this was perfect. She had just finished her first year as a lawyer, working in high finance. The deal she had just closed gave her a hefty commission and granted her the right to take a month-long vacation. That gave her all the time she needed to have the surgery and recover before she returned to the office as a new woman.

Candace had already gone over the mental challenges that would come with getting a breast augmentation. She had no doubt that everyone at work would figure it out, whether she shared the truth with them or not. However, she wasn't planning anything extreme. She just wanted to feel good about herself and feel normal. And any rumors or talk behind her back would die off eventually. Her work more than spoke for itself.

Choosing Thatcher Medical was a bit of a surprise. It was a little-known cosmetic surgery practice tucked away in the Pacific Northwest, not exactly the hotbed for breast augmentations. But Candace felt good about the virtual meeting she had with the surgeon and the before and after photos made it clear she was in great hands.

There was one other woman in the waiting room. She had fallen asleep, likely having traveled a great distance to be there. But even though they had been told to not bother with makeup and to avoid wearing constricting clothing, the other woman was decked out in what looked like a clubbing dress and sported a heavily made-up face, complete with bright pink lipstick.

"I guess getting a boob job is a bimbo right of passage," Candace muttered to herself. She looked down on the other woman with a degree of contempt. She had no respect for women who dolled themselves up and acted like a man's plaything.

Then again, Candace had nearly found herself in that situation. She fell for a man in her first year of university, hard. She would have done anything for him. Candace was ready to drop out and become his personal slut if he asked it of her. Luckily for her, he showed his true colors when she caught him in bed with another woman. Since then, Candace had been as serious as they came and it showed in her contempt for the other woman in the waiting room.

"Candi Summers?" A nurse stood in the doorway that led back to the pre-op room.

"It's Candace," she responded with a little bit of venom in her voice. Where had the nurse gotten Candi from?

Somehow Candace could tell Candi had been spelled with an i.

The nurse looked down at her chart, confusion on her face. But then she shrugged her shoulders. She didn't particularly care what the patients wanted to call themselves.

"It's time for your operation," the nurse said, covering for her mistake. "Follow me, please."

Candace shrugged off the mistake with her name and followed the nurse into the pre-op room. After that, it only took a few minutes before she was prepped and ready. By the time she was put under for the operation, she had reminded herself that she was in good hands and that when she woke up, everything would be perfect.

One reason that Candace chose Thatcher Medical for her surgery was the state of the art process that was supposed to significantly cut down on recovery time. She also liked how the clinic provided its own recovery ward where Candace could spend up to a month while she recovered from the surgery. The idea of being pampered like that was definitely attractive, regardless of the price. And even though she had only been working for a year, her success meant she could afford the best.

The moment Candace woke up, she knew something was wrong. She could almost feel it in her bones.

Top of the list was the pain. Candace expected some pain in her chest. After all, she had been opened surgically and two handfuls of silicone had been inserted. But there was more pain than just in her chest. Her face hurt, her scalp hurt, her throat hurt, her waist hurt, even her feet hurt.

Then there was the feeling of bandages on her face. She could even see them at the bottom of her vision. That made her wonder if she had been given a nose job in addition to her breast augmentation.

Or... Candace's thoughts started racing as she considered

other possibilities. Had she had a bad reaction to the anesthesia or the recovery drugs? That might explain the pain. But she didn't recall any warning about allergic reactions.

Candace tried calling out for help, but the moment she tried to use her vocal cords, piercing pain shot through her throat. She couldn't even groan in displeasure. She had been rendered mute, unable to communicate. And that fact scared her more than anything.

It was a rare day when Candace did not make her opinion known on one subject or another. She was not someone enamored with the sound of her own voice, but she was assertive and made sure to contribute to every conversation she was party to. It was part of who she was.

"Oh, you're awake." Candace glanced over to see a nurse walking into the room. It was a different nurse than the one who had helped admit her and prepare for surgery.

Candace wanted to scream out and ask what had happened to her, but there was no way for her to do so. The pain in her throat prevented her from speaking and her body hurt too much to move.

"The surgeries went just as expected," the nurse said, thinking she was comforting her patient. However, Candace became fixated on the plural of surgery. What else had they done to her? "I know you can't speak now, but the recovery drugs should have you feeling better in a few hours. It's probably for the best that you get some sleep. Before you know it, you'll feel better than ever. And that's when the real fun can start with the second part of your stay."

Panic raced through Candace as she took in the rest of the nurse's words. The second part of her stay? That made it sound like they had other operations planned for her, although she couldn't imagine going under the knife again so soon.

However, before Candace could get too caught up in

runaway fear, she spotted the nurse injecting something into her IV. A moment later sleep took her, washing away her worries.

When Candace woke up again, she immediately knew she felt better. She was aware that recovery time at Thatcher Medical had been significantly improved, but this seemed extreme. Then again, she had no idea how long she had been asleep. Time in general was a difficult concept after surgery and drug induced sleep.

However, now that the worst of the pain had receded, Candace was finally able to assess her situation. And the first thing she noticed was the bandages that had previously covered her nose and slightly obscured her vision were now gone. That seemed like a plus, but only until she looked down toward her chest.

After all, Candace had come to Thatcher Medical for a breast augmentation. But the moment she saw the two large mounds sticking off of her chest, she knew it had all gone wrong.

"This wasn't what I wanted," she complained, her ability to speak having returned to her. And it wasn't what she had wanted. Candace had simply wanted a small boost in size and to have her asymmetry fixed. But instead she had two large balloons stuffed under her skin.

But that wasn't all that had gone wrong. It took a moment for Candace's mind to register the change in her voice. It had come out at least an octave higher than it should have.

Candace raised a hand to her mouth, feeling the shock. But the moment her fingers touched her lips, she knew there was something else that had gone horribly wrong. Her lips were plump pillows, clearly enhanced.

"What the fuck?" Candace cried out, her voice making her sound almost childish. It sounded similar to how she had spoken around her ex from college. However, then it had been a conscious inflection. Now she couldn't help it.

Looking around the room, trying to figure out what else might be wrong, Candace found herself in a generic hospital recovery room. It was where she had expected to spend her recovery period. There was a mirror in the corner, but it didn't face in her direction.

"I have to see what they've done to me."

Candace pushed herself up to sitting. She could feel the weight of the large implants on her chest, more so now that they hung freely. Wasn't there supposed to be bandages and a surgical bra? Candace didn't let that question distract her as she swung her feet over the side of the bed.

Slipping down to the floor, pain shot up the back of Candace's legs the moment her bare feet touched the cold linoleum tiles. She grumbled, but the pain didn't stop her. She was determined to discover all that they had done to her.

Before taking her first step, Candace pulled the IV needle from her arm. Even if the stand was on wheels, it would just get in her way. An alarm sounded, but Candace ignored it as she stepped across the room.

The moment she caught sight of her reflection, Candace gasped in shock. The thin hospital smock did nothing to hide the giant protrusions on her chest. They completely dominated her figure, each breast being about as big as her head.

And speaking of her head, Candace could no longer recognize herself. Her lips were big and plump, clearly enhanced and clearly designed for a specific function, something that she had not done since that first year at university.

But it was more than just her lips. Her nose had clearly been altered, sculpted. It made her eyes look bigger, with longer lashes. Unless those had been altered too. It was hard to tell, but there was a definite doll-like quality to her face. And that was made all the more clear in the way her face barely moved. No matter what she did, her face remained almost expressionless, sitting somewhere between vapid cluelessness and resting bitch face. It was actually kind of hot.

Not that Candace let herself think for too long on the arousal forming at the sight of her own body. That was because there was so much more to consider. Top of the list was what rested at the top of her head. Her once short brown hair had been completely replaced by silky blonde locks that flowed down her back in loose waves. And it wasn't just any shade of blonde. It was platinum blonde.

"I look like a fucking bimbo."

"Look and sound," came a male voice. "There's just one more step and we'll have you thinking like one too."

Candace spun around to find a man in a white doctor's coat standing in the doorway. He showed no concern about her being out of bed, although once she recognized his presence, he walked over to the beeping medical machine and turned it off. The silence was welcome.

"I didn't want this." Candace wanted to scream, but she held back her anger, knowing it would add tension that could make her situation worse. "I was here for a small breast augmentation, not all of this." She motioned down her body with her hand, highlighting her breasts, her narrow waist, her expansive hips, and her long svelte legs that were on full display beneath the short hem of the smock.

The doctor stared at her for a moment, confusions slowly transforming to a sense of understanding on his face. "Now there."

He walked over to the foot of Candace's bed and grabbed the chart. He quickly looked at it, focusing on the top few lines.

"You're not Candi Summers, are you?"

"I'm Candace Summers. What's with you people thinking

my name is Candi? The nurse who admitted me called me Candi. I didn't understand. I don't understand what's going on."

"Yes, well there seems to have been a mistake. You see, in addition to the breast augmentation surgery scheduled for Candace Summers, we also had a bimbo transformation surgery scheduled for Candi Summers. You can see how this would cause a problem."

Horror would have dawned on Candace's face if her face could have shown such emotion. But the procedures that had been done to her left her face frozen, leaving her looking like a dumb bitch.

"You have to fix this." It was a simple demand, but as soon as those words left Candace's lips, she knew it wouldn't be that easy.

"We will," the doctor responded. "We'll make sure everything is taken care of. And I'll start on that right away."

Candace relaxed a little when the doctor left her room. She climbed back into bed and tried to rest. It was all she could do. And that task was made easier as a barely audible sound began to fill the room. Candace did not even realize that sound had been piped in. It only registered at an unconscious level, but it was effective nonetheless.

As soon as the doctor left Candace's room, he immediately went to his office and picked up the phone. Yes, a mistake had been made, but it was fixable. But how the clinic responded all had to do with the decision of one Roger Weatherholt, the sponsor of Candi Summers' bimbofication treatment. Did he want his original Candi or was he willing to accept the even hotter Candace?

After that, life for a Candace became oddly comforting. She lost huge swaths of time and found herself inwardly smiling the rest of the time as she came to terms with this new life. She could not actually smile as her face no longer showed emotion. But she was even learning to like that about her new self.

Each morning, afternoon, and evening Candace underwent a mental therapy session, slowly warping her mind, changing her reality, all of it unknown to the recovering woman. After her first week in the recovery room, she began masturbating between her sessions, her body always so turned on, both from the sight of her hyper-feminine form, but also at the thought of being an owned bimbo.

Such thoughts would have been hated before, but her resistance was wearing down, getting slowly chipped away with each session. And before she knew it, she was looking forward to her sessions, even if she did not understand what was happening, knowing each one made her less intelligent, more submissive, more complete, and a better bimbo.

When the recovery month had finished, she was a whole new woman. She knew this was her final day at Thatcher Medical and she wanted to celebrate by wearing the sexiest and hottest outfit she could manage.

The high heels were a given. The only time her heels ever held her weight was when she wore sky-high heels, her tendons and feet having been permanently altered.

The dress was white, highlighting the fact that she was a bimbo virgin, never having been fucked since becoming her new self. Although with several well placed cutouts, most of her body was on display, making it clear she wasn't wearing anything beneath the dress. Everyone who saw her would know exactly what kind of woman she was and that was how she wanted it.

Her face was heavily made up with pink lips that matched her long nails. Large hoop earrings graced her ears and nearly reached her shoulders. On one wrist she wore a watch with diamonds set into the face. Her other wrist was graced with several bangles to even out her perfectly symmetrical appearance.

Everything was ready. Her resignation had been recorded at the law firm where she had once worked. The doctors at the clinic had written it, but she had signed it without question. She didn't question anything anymore. She didn't know how.

Satisfied with her appearance, she blew her reflection a kiss before she walked out of her recovery room for the final time, ready to begin her new life.

"Candi."

The newly made bimbo squealed at the sight of Roger Weatherholt, although her face showed no emotion, as had been designed.

"Hi, Sir," Candi said, her voice turning seductive as she minced toward him. She wrapped an arm around the torso of the man she saw as her provider and owner, pressing herself against him, enjoying being reunited with her wealthy benefactor even though she had never actually met him before. She was his sugar baby.

But none of that mattered to the newly created Candi. Her past was forgotten. In her mind, she had never been anything other than a bimbo. And thanks to her Sir and the nice people at Thatcher Medical, she had the bimbo body to match her bimbo mind. It never occurred to her that she had ever been anything else.

A moment later, another woman appeared in the room. She was blonde, although there was a month's worth of dark roots showing. Her breasts were augmented, but not nearly as big as Candi's bimbolicious tits. And she looked groggy, like she had just woken up from a long nap. As it turned out, it had been a nearly month-long nap. This was the original Candi.

"Roger, what's going on?" the woman asked. "Who's that?"

Candi didn't wait for Roger to answer. "I'm his bimbo." Her words were laced with contempt for the poor excuse for a bimbo, having no idea that her treatment had originally been meant for the other woman.

"You bitch," the woman spat. Her whole life was suddenly ruined and she didn't understand why or how.

"That's right. I'm a bimbo bitch. I'm Sir's bimbo bitch. Now leave us alone. You could never be good enough for him." Candi looked up into Roger's eyes. "Isn't that right, Sir?"

"That's right, baby."

No more words were said as Roger led Candi out of the clinic and toward his car. Candi looked over her shoulder at the dejected woman she was leaving behind. She felt a sense of glee at the pain showing in the woman's eyes, the tears streaming down her cheeks. Who did that woman think she was to be deserving of the greatest man Candi could imagine?

The driver got an eyeful as he helped Candi into the backseat, but he didn't say anything. That was now one of the perks of his job. Roger joined her a moment later, sitting beside her in the back of the luxury car. And as the car pulled out into traffic, Candi used deft fingers to pull out Roger's cock so that she could wrap her plump lips around it, doing her bimbo duty.

The old Candi was left at the clinic to pick up the pieces of her life. She thought she had struck gold when Roger offered to turn her into his bimbo. Now she was forced to try to find another man who needed a wannabe bimbo like her. At least she still got bigger tits out of it, which would surely help as her journey in life continued.

As for the new Candi, she was happy as Roger's bimbo bitch. She never knew that this was her true calling in life, but she would never be left wanting again. Then again, her quieted mind made it so that as long as her basic needs were provided for and her access to cock was never taken from her, she would be the best bimbo bitch she could be. Sure, it had all been a mistake, but Candi wouldn't even complain if she could. This was the best life she could imagine now.

# WORDS HAVE POWER

Molly looked down at the screen, trying to guess what word it could be. She was late to the current online word game craze. But since the original game had been bought out, she had been looking for another version, something she felt better about playing.

That was what led Molly to playing Words Have Power. The simple interface and the ability to play it from anywhere, with or without an internet connection was perfect for her on-the-go lifestyle. And the makers of the game lacked the connections that made her squeamish about playing the original.

However, for the moment, Molly was home, dressed in a simple tank top and a pair of panties as she sat in bed, wanting to play the game before the clock ticked over into another day. She wanted to start her streak as soon as possible. And Molly was certain she would get a good streak going.

Five letters. That was what Molly needed to figure out. She needed five letters that formed a word.

FALSE

That was the word that Molly tried first. She entered the letters and pressed the guess button.

"Oh my," Molly said in surprise as she looked at what had come to her. She had not known what to expect with her first guess, but the F and the A were both in the right spots. That was huge.

It did not take long for Molly to make her second guess. Knowing the word started with an F and an A was a huge help.

FAIRY

Molly was not sure what to guess. She was not necessarily the best wordsmith around. If she had a dictionary, it would have been easier, but Molly knew that would be cheating.

"Three," Molly practically shouted. It was not just that she had three correct letters, but that they were in the right order. The first three letters of the word were F, A, and I. She just needed to figure out the last two.

Having always been jealous of the people who were able to answer these sorts of puzzles with two or three guesses, Molly really wanted to get the word right on her next guess. She wanted to start off playing the game with a win. But there was only one other word she could think of that was both five letters and started with those first three letters.

FAITH

That was Molly's third guess, but she was not sure she would be able to come up with an answer if it was wrong. She knew she was close. She just had to hope she had not missed anything.

The app dinged and Molly clutched the cross hanging from her neck, whispering a silent prayer of thanks. It had slipped out from the high neckline of her full-length pajamas.

"I did it," Molly finally said. Then she set her phone down on her nightstand, making sure it was on the charging pad. Then she picked up the Bible she always kept at her bedside to read a few passages before bed.

It was only the next morning that Molly realized something about her had changed. She had been in the middle of getting dressed, finding that her closet was filled with conservative clothes that always covered her knees and her shoulders. And yet, she specifically remembered going on a date once with a guy and getting a blob of mustard on her exposed chest. She had worn a low-cut top for her date, but she did not own any low-cut tops.

"Get a hold of yourself," Molly said as she braced herself against the dresser, two sets of memories filtering through her head. She distinctly remembered a past when she had not been religious. She remembered wearing a tank top and panties while she played the Words Have Power game. That Molly had been an atheist. But she also now remembered being devout and never wavering from her religious beliefs.

It was only then that Molly understood what had happened. It was the game. Her word had been faith and now she was a woman of faith. The word had power.

Under normal circumstances, that probably would have been enough for Molly to stop playing the game. She already recognized that the game had a transformative power over her. And yet, when she climbed into bed the next night, having said a prayer, but before she finished off the night with a Bible passage reading, Molly opened the Words Have Power app and started to play.

STUDY

That was Molly's opening guess. She had been thinking about Bible Study and how much meaning she got out of every meeting. Molly knew that had not always been the case, but she had a hard time caring. Her past and her present might not sync, but she would live her current life as best as she could and, for the moment, that meant she was a devout religious woman who regularly attended Bible Study.

And to Molly's delight, she had guessed well to start. The S was in the right place and there was also a T in the word, although it was not in the second position. She just needed to figure out what to try next.

Molly knew her next guess was wrong, but she could not think of anything better at the moment. So she put her guess in and hoped for the best.

START

The first T was in the wrong place, but it had two new letters to try with.

"Oh, thank you," Molly quickly prayed, unwilling to take her god's name in vain. It was the wrong word, but she now had four letters in the right place. The opening S was the same, but the A, R, and the second T were all in the right place.

SMART

Molly did not even need to think very hard on that one. She plugged in the first word she could think of that made sense and for the second day in a row, she had guessed correctly.

The Bible disappeared from Molly's bedside. So too did the cross around her neck. Her clothing returned to the tank top and panties she had worn to bed previously. In fact, just about everything had returned to what it had been before she had started playing Words Have Power. But there were a few differences. One wall of Molly's apartment now included the various academic awards and degrees she had obtained. She was smart. Molly was very smart. Even though she was still relatively young, she had acquired multiple doctorate degrees and been published in numerous prestigious journals.

But none of that mattered at the moment, because Molly was very aware that she needed to go to bed. Sleep was one of the ways she kept her brain firing on all cylinders. It was how she maximized her intelligence. She turned out the light and went to sleep, her mind dreaming up her latest great idea.

Molly had never understood before how her life could be improved with an increase in intelligence. Everything came to her more easily now. When faced with a situation, she could automatically figure out a solution, barely having to think about it.

But with greater intelligence also came greater responsibility. Molly found her job to be completely different. That should have been expected. With multiple doctorates, she could not expect to be in the same role as before. Molly worked for the same company, a large multinational conglomerate, but instead of working in a cubicle on the third floor, she had both an office, with a view, and a laboratory, where she worked on the cutting edge of science and technology. But the office meant she was also managing people, a whole department in fact.

By this point, at the end of the day when Molly was back at home and thinking about how to occupy herself, there was a part of her that wanted to just walk away from the Words Have Power game, knowing that whatever word she got would be the new her. Molly's genius level intellect would evaporate and she would become someone else. However, Molly could not back down from an intellectual challenge. There was no way she could leave the game alone.

Sitting in bed, having already read several articles in a scientific journal, Molly opened the Words Have Power app to begin the day's challenge. She already knew she had several good guesses she could make. She could easily work out the probabilities and statistics of each starting word. And then she made her choice.

CRANE

Molly liked that word, because it included the two most common vowels and several common consonants. It was not necessarily the perfect word, but it worked for her needs. However, it turned out not to be a good starting word for the day's puzzle. Only the C was present in the word of the day, but not in the first position.

Sitting back, Molly considered her options. Her word needed to have a C in it. Other than that, she needed to find additional letters to remove from consideration. The only way to do that was to choose a word with other common letters in it, especially a T.

Molly glanced up at her wall. In the place of the photographs of events with friends on the wall, there was a large world map. Not only was Molly curious about science and technology, but she was also curious about the world in general, both in terms of geography and different cultures.

DUTCH

It was an impulsive choice, but it included the C and it included a T.

"Goed," Molly said as she celebrated guessing correctly, unintentionally speaking Dutch and not English. It had only taken her two tries to get the word. Only now she had lost the genius-level intellect she had been graced with previously and had instead been given a Dutch background. Suddenly Molly could remember growing up in The Netherlands and moving to the United States during high school. She spoke English, but there was a slight accent that still remained. If anything, she sounded more British than American, since her English was learned back at home and not in the States.

There was a part of Molly that was relieved not to have all that responsibility anymore, but she did miss the extra brain power. However, she had a hard time denying the enjoyment she had from being a multinational person. Being bilingual did not hurt either. It certainly impressed her friends and work colleagues.

Without a way to change her situation, she set her phone aside and turned out the light, going to bed. Yet despite her determination to sleep, she was excited for what the app would next give her.

The next day had been entirely average. Sure, she had a Dutch background, but that had not changed her job or the position she held previous to becoming extra smart. The only difference was that she was occasionally asked to repeat herself, because someone did not understand her light accent.

As soon as Molly arrived home, she changed out of her work clothes, instead choosing a comfortable tank top and a pair of loose-fitting jeans. But as she sat down on her couch, she decided to play Words Have Power instead of immediately turning on the television.

CRAMP

That was Molly's first guess. She no longer had the intellect to make the game easy for her. But she had luck with words that started with C originally.

As it turned out, she only had one letter right and it was in the wrong place. There was an M, but not in the fourth position. She had to think hard about what word she wanted to try next.

MESTO

Molly was not sure what the word meant, but she was pretty sure she had heard it before. And the app accepted it as a viable word, so it had to work. And as luck would have it, she got more information out of it. The M was still in the wrong place, but the O was in the right spot. She was getting closer.

GUMBO

Molly had always liked various food dishes from different regions of the world and gumbo was one of her favorites, even though she had no connection to Louisiana or the cultures that influenced the cuisine. But now Molly knew she was getting close. She had three letters right. Not only were M, B, and O in the word, but they were in the right places too.

LIMBO

Knowing how easy the game had been yesterday, Molly was a little annoyed at how long this puzzle was taking her, but she was still making progress. LIMBO had been a good guess and she now had the I, M, B, and O in the right positions. But she had yet to solve the puzzle.

Molly went through the letters the word could start with. There were limits, given the letters she had ruled out already. She decided to try K.

KIMBO

Words Have Power did not like that. KIMBO was not a word the game recognized. Then Molly realized the word she was looking for was akimbo. But that had six letters. She blamed her Dutch background. She might have been able to speak what sounded like flawless English, but there were words she still did not know

"Oh no," Molly said, suddenly realizing what the word had to be. There was only one word left. And as much as there was a part of Molly that was happy to no longer have all the responsibility that her previous genius-level intellect had given her, she also did not want to go the other direction.

Hoping to not play, Molly tried to close out of the app. Except her phone did not seem to let her. Molly then turned off the screen, hoping that could fix things, but as soon as she turned the phone back on, it went right to the game. The app had taken over her phone.

"It's just one day," Molly told herself as she debated what to do next. All it would take was for her to solve the next day's puzzle and then she would no longer be a bimbo anymore. That seemed reasonable. And who knew? Molly might even enjoy herself for her day as a bimbo. It was worth a shot.

BIMBO

The moment Molly submitted her guess, her whole world changed in a flash. She looked down and was greeted with an impressive display of cleavage. Two big and round tits stuck off her chest as her top did almost nothing to hide them. The wide neckline dropped all the way to her sternum. It was obvious to everyone that she was not wearing a bra, but with such obviously fake tits, a bra was not needed. They stood up all by themselves.

But it was not just Molly's body that had so obviously changed. And there had been a lot of changes, transforming her body into a man's wet dream, clearly designed for sex and for turning people on. It was Molly's mind that changed. Her thoughts went from moving at a normal rate through her mind and slowed to a crawl, as if they were swimming upstream in a river of molasses. There was a blankness in her eyes that simply could not otherwise be explained.

Molly's whole life had been rewritten. The memories of her past selves still existed, but they were filed away in places she no longer seemed to want to access. She could barely remember what she did yesterday. If there was not a selfie on her phone of the occasion, she largely forgot. Such was Molly's emphasis on living in the present. And at the present, Molly was trying to figure out which club she wanted to go to.

Posing in front of her mirror, Molly took in all of her perfect bimbo form. Her hourglass figure was aided by her fake tits and her bubble butt. The narrow waist came from careful eating and lots of exercise. Her lips had recently been plumped up with another round of filler. Molly could not get enough of that stuff. Her lips barely closed anymore with an almost permanent keyhole pout. But it was the blank eyes and long mane of platinum blonde hair that really sold it that she was a complete bimbo. It took an incredible amount of effort to maintain her appearance, but it was worth it in her mind.

Molly pushed out her chest and made a kissing face as she snapped another picture. She was always taking selfies. However, her phone beeped and gave her a warning that there was not enough storage space on her phone for any more photos. She needed to clear up space.

"Phooey," Molly said, her voice high pitched and breathy. It was not that her voice had changed, but she had trained herself to speak differently over the years, to sound more like the vapid airhead that she portrayed. Had Molly wanted to search her memories, she might have discovered that she had not always been this way. But she had trained herself to be the perfect example of what men wanted in a woman. And that included training her voice until she naturally spoke that way.

But the question of what Molly would remove from her phone posed a problem. It required making a decision and she was so used to letting other people make her decisions for her that she struggled with even the most basic choices, unless they revolved around sex or fashion. Those were the only two areas where Molly could consider herself an expert.

Molly started looking through her phone, trying to decide what could go. The idea of deleting any of her pictures seemed like blasphemy, even if it would eventually come to that. Instead, she looked at the apps. The news app that came native with the phone was an easy one to get rid of. Same for the weather app. If Molly wanted to know what the weather was, all she needed to do was look out the window.

But while she was on the subject of deleting apps, Molly came across the game Words Have Power. Deep down, she knew that the app was the reason she was now a bimbo. She also knew that it had the power to transform her life. Except Molly loved her life. She got to focus on looking sexy and getting guys, and even a few women, to fuck her. Her life was filled with pleasure. And besides, it was not like she could even think of words to make as guesses. Word puzzles were not her thing.

"Bye bye," Molly said as she deleted the Words Have Power app. It was technically not permanent, but it gave Molly a sense of satisfaction when it was gone. Or maybe it was just the fact that she now had enough room to take that selfie she had wanted to take.

Molly once again posed in front of her full-size mirror, pushing out her chest and making an exaggerated kissing face. When the camera on her phone snapped her photo, she smiled. She looked so sexy in the picture.

Molly immediately swiped over to her social media account with her long-nailed fingers and uploaded the picture. She played with the filters for a few minutes, wanting to make herself look as sexy as possible. She could not remember how many social media accounts she had gotten banned on, often forgetting that she needed to tone down her overt sexuality. But that was not an issue this time. She was scantily clad, as she always was, but everything was covered.

"Heading to the Lucky Seven," Molly typed out, managing to spell everything correctly. "Looking for a hookup."

That was all that needed to be said. Molly had fucked her followers before. Tonight was going to be no different.

With her phone placed safely in her clutch purse, Molly wiggled and jiggled toward the door, her high heels forcing her ass to sway from side to side. It was going to be a good night. But for Molly, now that she was a bimbo, every night was a good night.

# THE CAR BIMBO

"Whoa, I'm surprised they let a girl in here that wasn't one of the car models."

Lucia bristled at the man's comment. Even though she had been getting comments like that ever since she showed up at her first car show, they still hurt. Too many men saw her as an outsider, somehow believing that the automotive world was exclusively male. They were the same men who complained about women race car drivers.

"Look, dude," Lucia started, although she had yet to come up with what she planned to say next. She had never been good at comebacks.

But before Lucia could continue, the man held up his hand and somehow that silenced her. She wanted to tell him off for being an ass, but she found herself incapable of making a sound. It was not that she was physically unable to speak, but there seemed to be a strange disconnect between her brain and her mouth. However, that only made it worse, because panic started to well up inside of her.

"Stay calm," the man said. "I think we need to have a little chat. Follow me over to my car."

Lucia inexplicably found herself calming down as she followed the man over toward a yellow muscle car. Even if she could explain how she had suddenly become calm and even docile, she could not explain why she followed him. Worse, if his car was any signal of his taste, she knew the two of them would not get along. Lucia was more interested in European sports cars. They might not be as powerful, but they applied their power to the road much better. The types of cars she preferred were ones that could go fast and turn without crashing.

The man stopped in front of his car and Lucia stopped beside him. She hated the idea that she even looked like she was having a normal conversation with this guy. She might have been calm about it, but that did not mean she had to like it. But as much as she wanted to walk away, she found her legs unwilling to move. She was stuck until the man dismissed her. And she did not even know his name.

"You know, I bet you'd be pretty hot if you actually tried," the man said as he looked Lucia up and down. She was dressed in a simple T-shirt and jeans with a pair of work boots on her feet. She was generally uninterested in fashion or appealing to the male eye. Sure, her interests put off most guys, but she was certain she would find the right man for her eventually. And if she failed at that, it was no bother for her. She could handle life as a single female car enthusiast.

"Oh, that's right, I silenced you," the man said. He did not mention how he had done it, which irritated Lucia, but at least he was aware of the power he seemed to have over her. "You can speak, but only when spoken to. And nothing mean-spirited. A girl like you should be smiling, both inside and out."

"Thank you." Those were the only words Lucia was able to speak. She wanted to say so much more, but the man had prevented her from saying more somehow. Worse, she found her spirits lifting. She was already surprisingly calm, but now she actually felt happy. The corners of her lips turned up into the slightest smile.

"Now where are my manners? My name is Brett. What's your's?"

"Lucia." It was a simple answer for a simple question. Lucia did not want to give Brett her name, but as soon as the question was asked, she found herself answering it without even thinking about it.

"Lucia, that's a nice name," Brett said. The more that Lucia looked at him, the more she noticed his strong jaw and the corded muscles on his arms. She could guess his chest and abs were equally as impressive. He was tall and strong, with a deep voice and almost kind eyes. They were almost kind, because despite the fact they looked genuinely good, Brett's power of her seemed far less kind. "But I bet a girl like you prefers to go by Lulu."

"Yes, please call me Lulu."

And just like that, Lucia now thought of herself as Lulu. She had no idea where the name had come from. She had never heard anyone call her that before, but she suddenly had memories of people using her nickname instead of her real name.

"And I bet a girl like you prefers it so much that you got your name changed legally. Got to have the driver's license match the real you."

Without even thinking about it, Lulu reached into her back pocket and pulled out her license. Sure enough, it had her nickname on it, not her given name. Lulu could hardly believe she would have done that, but the proof was right there in front of her eyes.

"So what brings you to the car show today?" Brett asked. At least he seemed genuinely curious, leaving Lulu to actually be happy about answering him.

"I have always had a thing for cars," Lulu found herself explaining. "The mechanics and engineering of them fascinate me. I'm not interested in the culture around them. I just like to see the sleek lines and to get a chance to look under the hood."

There was silence for a moment after Lulu finished speaking. Brett was considering his words carefully, but Lulu was unable to speak up. She had answered his question and she would remain quiet until she was spoken to again.

"I suppose cars like these get you hot," Brett finally said. "I bet you could orgasm from the revving of an engine or the vibrations as they flow through the car when you're sitting in the passenger seat."

It was like a switch was flipped in Lulu's head. One moment she cared about cars from a mechanical perspective. The next moment she loved them because they made her horny and could even make her cum. It did not make sense, but Lulu could feel it. All of these cars parked out on the grass in this park were making her uncomfortably wet and horny. Her panties were already soaked.

"You have a question for me, I'm guessing," Brett said. "Go ahead and ask it."

"How?" Lulu asked. "How are you doing this to me?"

"It's my gift," Brett answered. "I can speak things into existence. I take what I see and I craft it with my words and change it, transform it. And you, my horny little car slut, are going to be my prize for the weekend. We're going to have so much fun, don't you think?"

"No," Lulu blurted out. "Can't you leave me alone?"

Brett chuckled as he slowly shook his head. "You don't get it, do you? You have no power here. But I'll make you a deal. I'll let you help choose what happens to you. Otherwise, you get my choices and I have a feeling you won't like them. Then again, you won't have the power to not like them when I'm done with you."

Lulu stood there and tried to think. She was already starting to get confused about what was real and what he had changed about her. She knew her name was Lulu, but even that was fuzzy on whether she had decided to go with her nickname full-time or if he had given it to her. But she knew she was a car slut. She came to these shows to hook up with car owners, more because she got off on their machines as opposed to the men. There was something special about sucking a guy off as he drove down the road or getting him to pull over so she could ride him, hopefully with the engine still running.

"Like what do you mean?" Lulu finally asked, not sure what he meant. Could she really decide what to change about herself? That seemed ridiculous. How could she even choose?

"Let's say you actually dress like the slut you are instead of those boring clothes that no man could find hot. Let's get you in some high heels, and tiny shorts and a cropped top."

Lulu looked down and for the briefest of moments, she recognized that her clothes were changing. But then she blinked and she saw the clothing she had worn to the car show. Sure, the revealing clothing was a bit much for some of the prudish men who cared more about every part in every car being original than how good the cars looked, how good they sounded, and how much they made her drip with arousal. Lulu dressed like a slut so that she could make sure the receptive men, like Brett, would be sure to give her a chance.

"But of course I'm dressed this way," Lulu said. "Would you want to fuck me if I was wearing a boring and shapeless sweater?"

"Well, how would you make yourself look like a bigger

slut?" Brett asked. "Humor me and let's see what you can come up with."

"I guess I'd be fitter," Lulu said, placing her hand on her exposed midriff. She had an extra layer of fat there that she had been trying to get rid of for a year with no success.

"You are fitter," Brett said and suddenly her body tightened overall. It was not just the improved look of her midriff, but her whole body gained both muscle tone and stamina. That also helped in the sex department, allowing her to twist her body into more positions, making sure that no car could keep her from getting what she needed from the man inside with her.

"Do you think my breasts could be bigger?" Lulu asked. "I've never understood why guys are fixated on breasts, but I suppose that could help."

"You have extra large implants to give you big, round, bolted-on tits with prominent nipples," Brett said. "And while I'm at it, you've also had significant lip filler to give you cocksucking lips and even had butt implants for the perfect bubble butt."

Lulu wanted to be angry, but then she looked down and got a little lost in her own exposed cleavage. Her whole body almost instantly shifted. One moment she looked like a slut, but one who had achieved her status through entirely natural means. Now there was no question of what kind of woman Lulu was. She was a plastic slut, completely willing to go under the knife or receive injections to give her body the appropriate proportions. She wanted to look a certain way and made sure that she did so, regardless of the cost.

"I'm guessing that the money for all that surgery didn't come through a normal job," Brett continued. "Stripping and even a little escorting was how you paid for that smoking hot body of yours."

Lulu found her life getting rewritten before she could

even realize what was changing. Her past shifted. She started stripping to pay for college. But then she saw all the plastic strippers and how much money they made and how hot they were and she then worked extra hard to pay for her own upgrades. Her classmates thought she was crazy and maybe even a gender traitor, but Lulu was hooked. And then when a man came into the club, having parked his fancy sports car in the parking lot, she quickly learned that cars turn her on more than men. The rest was history.

"Yes, that's much better," Brett said. "See? You've already been a great help." Lulu beamed at the compliment, although she still did not understand what he was talking about. "But let's see if we can't keep things going here. You're so close to perfect."

"I mean, I guess my hair could be longer and thicker, you know? And, um, I'm sorry, it's kind of hard to think right now. All these cars, they turn me on."

Brett smiled. "Of course. I know just what you need. You've got long voluminous hair." Lulu's dark hair grew out and gained in volume until it reached the small of her back. It looked a little unkempt, but that was more to play up the slut angle. "And you're pretty much a bimbo. Thinking is hard so you don't trouble yourself with it. You let men, especially men who drive fast cars with big engines, make the decisions for you."

Lulu could only stand there as her mind emptied. She had once known every major component in a car. Now she would giggle uncontrollably if someone mentioned a camshaft, thinking they were talking about a cock instead. But that did not stop her from getting turned on by cars. And she was pretty sure Brett had a fast and powerful car. She wouldn't know for sure until he revved the engine and she felt the vibrations in her pussy, but she was pretty sure she could get him to do that for her. She was a slut after all.

However, before Lulu could speak, Brett took the lead. "Now that we've got all of that figured out, how about you and I go take my car for a spin? The show is close to being over and I bet you horny bimbo car slut like you could use a good hard fucking."

"Yes, please," Lulu squealed. She was already waiting at the passenger door when Brett arrived to open it for her. She knew better than to touch a man's car without permission.

A moment later, Brett had joined her in the car. And the moment the engine turned over and he revved it, she knew she had made the right decision. The vibrations nearly made her cum. And she was sure that she would cum before they got to wherever Brett was taking her. But for Lulu, it was not the destination that mattered, it was all about the ride and all the fucking along the way. She was a bimbo and a car slut and she was rolling down the open highway of life, enjoying every moment of it.

# DEALING WITH THE HEAT

"It's so hot," Ruby complained as she tried to fan herself to get even the smallest amount of airflow over her skin.

The trip was supposed to be the time of her life. Traveling with her boyfriend, Sam, was supposed to be the final step before he finally proposed. Ruby thought he might before the trip was over, but that was before the heat wave hit. Their hotel room lacked air conditioning and there seemed to be no way to keep the heat out. It was too hot to go out and explore the city, but it was also too hot to just sit around in their dark hotel room.

"Yeah," Sam agreed. He sat in a chair, just wearing a pair of boxer shorts. Sweat beaded on his skin. He seemed to be coping with the heat just as badly as Ruby was.

The problem with the heat was how all-encompassing it was. It was almost impossible to think about anything else.

"I'm gonna go see if the ice machine has any ice now," Ruby said as she pushed herself back up to her feet. She was dressed a bit more modestly, wearing a loose tank top and a pair of nylon running shorts. It definitely was not a sexy look, but Ruby was too hot to even try to pull off sexy. She was just going for survival.

Sam waved goodbye to his girlfriend, knowing that she would either return with sweet relief or they would be in the same boat that they now found themselves in. The sweltering heat was abnormal, even for the height of summer. That was what everyone told them. But just because the heat was abnormal, and a clear signal that climate change was already here, that did not mean that it was any easier to deal with.

Ruby slipped her sandals onto her feet and headed out into the main hallway of the boutique hotel. The hallway was no cooler. If anything, it was worse, because the air was stagnant. The heat, coupled with the humidity, made it feel as if Ruby was fighting to just move through the air.

She had been going out to check on the ice machine every hour. Whatever ice it was producing was being snatched up by other guests. But this time, when she reached the machine, it had a big "Out of Order" sign stuck to it. It had even been pulled out away from the wall, making it clear that it was not in operating condition.

Ruby sighed, knowing that this whole situation was partly her fault. Sam had originally booked them into modern hotels, chains similar to those that operated elsewhere, but Ruby had insisted on a more authentic experience. That meant small boutique hotels.

And that had worked great at first. The added character made up for the slight inconveniences they had experienced thus far. But now with the heat, they were both paying for Ruby's demands. Sam had already tried to get a room with a hotel that had air conditioning, but they were already booked out. Locals were renting rooms to escape the heat as well as other tourists. They were out of luck.

Just before Ruby trudged back to the room, she walked a little farther along the hallway toward the office. She figured she could at least inquire about when the ice machine might be fixed. Knowing her luck, it would be right after she and Sam checked out, but if there was hope to be had, that was where it would come from.

"Hot enough for you?" the clerk in the office asked in heavily accented English.

"This is hotter than back at home for me," Ruby answered. "And we routinely get hot weather. But I've never felt anything like this before. It all seems so hopeless."

The clerk nodded his head. It was unclear how well he understood English. He could speak it well enough to be understood, but that did not mean he had a good ear for it.

"I wanted to ask about the ice machine," Ruby continued.

"It's broken for at least a week."

Ruby's shoulders slumped at the news. They would be gone by then, but so too would the heat. Whatever the problem was with the ice machine, it was not about to get fixed anytime soon.

But before Ruby turned to go back to the room, she noticed that the clerk seemed to be completely unfazed by the heat. He sat behind his desk, perusing who knew what on his computer, wearing a heavy long sleeve shirt. It almost looked like he had been cold.

"How are you not sweating in this heat?" Ruby asked, exasperated and at her wits end.

"Me?" the man said. "I don't know what you're talking about."

"And those clothes. It's like you're actually cold. How? I'm barely able to function in this heat. My boyfriend is upstairs sitting in his underwear because of this heat."

Ruby assumed the clerk would shrug her off and he would let it all remain a mystery. But just as he started to lift his shoulders in a shrug, he instead reached and opened a drawer in the desk and pulled out a small pill bottle.

"These are my secret," he said. "I don't normally share, but I feel bad for you and your boyfriend. One each will have you both feeling cool and up for anything for the rest of the day."

Ruby was certain the man's offer was quackery. There were no pills like that. They were more likely to be illicit drugs, ecstasy or some sort of opiate. But Ruby was also desperate.

The man said nothing as he opened the bottle and tapped out two pills into his hand. Then he held them out for Ruby to take from him. She snatched them up, almost as if she was being given something that could be taken away from her at any moment.

"One is all you need," he said. "Too much can cause problems."

Ruby popped one of the pills into her mouth and swallowed it dry.

"Thanks," she said before she walked out of the office.

The walk back to the room was painfully hot. Her top was soaked through with sweat by the time she reached the door to their room. She looked down into her hand and wondered if she should share the pill or not. Sam deserved to feel cool, but she felt like she was close to passing out. It was that hot.

"Fuck it," Ruby said as she popped the second pill into her mouth and swallowed it dry. She did not need to tell Sam. At least one of them would start to feel better.

It was only when Ruby opened the door and found Sam sitting there, unmoved from when she left him, that she started to feel guilty about her actions. But she was already starting to feel relief. The heat, while still present, started to become more manageable. The pills were working. Or at least the first one was. It was too soon for the second to have kicked in, but Ruby was now confident that she would be one cool cucumber soon enough.

"Any luck?" Sam asked.

"The machine is now out of order and it won't be repaired until after we check out. We're out of luck."

"Fuck."

Ruby went over to the window and pulled back the curtain that was keeping the sun out of the room. She looked out onto the empty street below. It would have been picturesque if it were not so hot.

When Ruby turned around, she saw Sam staring at her.

"What?" she asked, confused. But when a giggle escaped her lips, she too knew something was wrong. She never giggled.

"You're breasts, they're bigger."

Ruby looked down to see the twin peaks that had become her breasts push out against the tank top she wore. She looked down into an expanse of cleavage that she had never had before. And yet, as she looked down, seeing her hard nipples tent the fabric on the tips of her tits, despite the heat, she felt as if what she now saw was right. This was how she was supposed to be. She just never knew that before.

"Mmm," Ruby moaned as she brought her hands up to her tits and cupped the undersides, almost like she was presenting them to Sam. "And they feel so good. Do you want to touch my boobies?"

Sam had no idea how to respond to his girlfriend's words or the way she reacted to the sudden growth of her tits. And at their new size, they were definitely tits. There was no way that any of the bras she brought with her on the trip would fit her now, not even her sports bra. But then again, the way her tits pushed off her chest, almost as if they had been bolted on, she did not really need a bra. They stood up just fine without one.

Ruby's gaze moved from her cleavage to Sam where she saw his cock straining against his boxers. She had to admit he looked really sexy sprawled out on the chair like that, sweat glistening on his skin, highlighting his muscles. She giggled again, laughing at nothing in particular. Her mind seemed so slow, which on its own seemed to be giggle worthy. It was like everything she thought she knew, about herself, about life, was wrong. What had once made sense now made no sense and the only way for her to respond to that was by giggling.

Sam pushed himself out of his seat and stepped toward his girlfriend, his eyes drinking in her now exaggerated form. Even the short time it took to cross the distance between his chair and his girlfriend, he noticed how Ruby's tits had continued to grow. Whatever was happening to her was continuing. However, rather than worry, his cock took charge, approving of everything that seemed to be happening to her.

And it was only when he approached, when Sam almost stood over her, that he noticed it was not just her tits that were growing. Her ass was filling out as well, stretching the shorts she wore until they were tight across her backside. It was the kind of bubble butt that either required years of hard work in the gym or spending thousands of dollars on a surgeon. Ruby got it without either.

There was no way that Sam was going to complain at the sudden increased hotness of his girlfriend. He loved her no matter what, but whatever was happening to her was turning her into the girl of his wet dreams. Her tits stretched her top, forcing it to slide up her taut midriff, revealing several inches of bare skin. He placed his hands on her exposed hips and pushed them up and under her top until his hands reached the undersides of her tits.

"Yeah, baby," Ruby moaned, lost in how good Sam's hands felt on her body. She was more aroused than she could ever remember being before, having now idea that her libido had grown with the size of her tits and ass, giving her a new baseline that would always keep her wet and ready for action.

But it was not just Ruby's tits and ass that were growing. Her lips got a similar treatment, pushing out from her face, gaining in both volume and projection, until it was clear they served a simple, yet specific, purpose. They were cocksucking lips. And that fact was made even more clear she her little pink tongue darted out and wetted her lips, in what turned into an erotic display that only served to turn Sam on all the more, making his shaft solid.

"I don't understand what's happening to you, but I need to fuck you right now," Sam said.

It only took a moment for him to pull Ruby's tank top up and over her head. She raised her arms to allow him full access to her body. He tossed the top across the room, discarding it, because she would not be needing it again for a while. But once she was topless, Sam stepped back so that he could get a complete look at her tits. They were absolutely massive now and looked far too big and round to be real. But they looked amazing with a flawless tan sweeping over her skin, giving her a sun kissed appearance.

What neither Sam nor Ruby noticed as he stepped forward again and started tugging on her shorts was that Ruby's intelligence was sinking like a stone. She had been a woman of above average intelligence, but those days were now behind her. Her eyes lost some of their focus, her thoughts slowing down to such an extent that she was quickly going to find it easier to giggle and twirl her hair in response to being asked a question.

Once Ruby stepped out of her shorts, her bare pussy on complete display, Sam led her over to the bed so that he could finally fuck her. The couple had had sex before. That was not new. However, they had never had sex while Ruby looked like a sex doll. Everything about her body had become perfect. Her skin was taut, her body perfectly sculpted with an hourglass figure that Sam had never imagined Ruby being able to have. And with her mind out of the way, she had become his perfect sexy bimbo girlfriend, constantly ready to fuck.

And fuck they did. Sam ignored the heat, pushed on by another kind of heat entirely, as he fucked her in every way imaginable. He took her from behind, enjoying the view of her bubble butt. He took her as she laid on her back, enjoying the way her tits stood up off her chest. He even fucked her mouth, putting her plump lips to good use.

But when Sam was finally spent, when his cock could no longer stay up, when the heat in their little hotel room had finally gotten the best of him, he fell back onto the bed, collapsing under the strain he had put himself through. Ruby, on the other hand, was a bundle of energy. She paid no attention to the sweltering heat as she bounced around the room, her mind flitting from one thing to another, never staying on topic or task for very long. She searched through her suitcase, looking for a sexy outfit to wear, but struggling to find anything that fit her new body and her new sense of style.

The knock at the door barely roused Sam from where he laid on the bed, but Ruby was more than happy to answer the door, not bothering to cover her sexy body in the slightest.

"Hi," Ruby said, her voice at least an octave higher than it had been before. The man at the door was the clerk, the same man from the hotel office who had given her the pills.

"I wanted to come in and check on you two," the clerk said, his eyes never leaving Ruby's tits and her pointy nipples. "I heard the sex from down the hall. I hoped that meant you were both feeling better."

However, the clerk managed to drag his gaze away from Ruby's body to see the exhausted form of Sam on the bed. He knew right away what had happened. The vapid smile on Ruby's face would have been enough to make it clear, even without her big tits drawing in the eye. She had taken both of the pills he had provided, despite the warning he had given her. Now, she was a bimbo, in body and in mind, permanently. And Sam was still overheated and likely in need of a cold drink of water.

The clerk pushed past Ruby and entered the room, knowing she would have let him in if he had asked. She would not have known not to, just like she did not know that she should have answered the door after covering herself up first.

"Here, you're going to need this," the clerk said as he pulled out the pill bottle and tapped out another little gem. He pushed the little pill into Sam's mouth and then held his head up as he gave him a drink of water from a glass on the nightstand.

The clerk's pill would help Sam recover from the heat, but the exhaustion Sam felt would still take time to recover from. But the clerk intended to stay until he had.

The clerk sat down in the chair that Sam had previously vacated. He then snapped his fingers, getting Ruby's attention, and then pointed at his crotch.

Ruby shot across the room in a flash, her tits bouncing unrestrained, before she sank to her knees and deftly freed the clerk's cock. Then she wrapped her plump lips around his shaft.

As Ruby happily sucked on the clerk's cock, she never once thought about the fact that she was technically cheating on her boyfriend. Such a concept of cheating or monogamous relationships were now lost on her. Ruby was a bimbo who understood her purpose. Her reason for being was to make cocks hard and then milk them for every drop of cum she could. Sam was still recovering, but there was another cock she could serve.

Sam and Ruby's stay at the hotel would prove to be an important one, but in the end, they were both guaranteed to be happier for choosing the boutique hotel over something more modern. Sam never worried about popping the question and proposing to Ruby, but she was happy to have him to guide her in her new life. Sam had a bimbo at his beck and call and Ruby could focus on what she did best, being the sexiest bimbo she could be.

# ABOUT THE AUTHOR

Sadie Thatcher is a longtime author of erotic fiction, especially related to transformations and bimbofication. She likes to say "I have thrown off the shackles of my conservative upbringing and now write erotic stories."

She maintains a special blog devoted to her writings, including a behind the scenes look at her writing process, and bimbos in general, as well as highlights works by other authors. They can be found at:

https://authorsadiethatcher.tumblr.com

The Bimbo Professor: The Curse of Playing Bimbo Tag Book 3

Anything for the Job

Anything for the Job 2

Anything for His Job

The Bimbo in the Mirror

The Bimbo in the Mirror 2

Astrid and the Bimbo Bee

Bella and the Bimbo Bee

Cali and the Bimbo Bee

Desiree and the Bimbo Bee

Ember and the Bimbo Bee

Fiona and the Bimbo Bee

The Intern

The Lawyer

The Hacker

Cause & Effect

Witless Protection

Stealing Sally

Trial and Error

Beta Testing

Exposed

Bimbo for a Weekend

Bimbo for a Week

Bimbo for Life

Fake It Until You Make It Season 1

Fake It Until You Make It Season 2

Simple and Fun Volume 1

Simple and Fun Volume 2

Simple and Fun Volume 3

Simple and Fun Volume 4

Simple and Fun Volume 5

Simple and Fun Volume 6

Bimbo Halloween

Bimbo Christmas

Bimbo Technology

Dorm Room Bimbo

Carissa's Magic Pen

Spirit Walk

Muscle Memory

The Case of the Bimbo Wife

Changes

Changes 2

New Year New You

The Bimbo Dream

The Wedding Gift

The Cure

Backfire

Bim & Bo Yoga

Wishing for Each Other

Bimbo Roots

A Bimbo at Oktoberfest

The Lost Bet

The Fountain

Bimbo Ghost

Sugar and Spice and Everything Nice

Basic Bimbo

Body Swap Rings: Happy Anniversary

Body Swap Rings 2: Wedding Night

The Bimbo Experience

The Bimbo Experience 2

The Bimbo Experience 3some

The 4th Bimbo Experience

Bimbo Genes

Bimbo Genes II: The Virus

The Bimbo Genes III: The Epidemic

Bimbo Juice: Blue Raspberry

Bimbo Juice: Grape

Bimbo Juice: Mango

Bimbo Juice: Pineapple

Bimbo Juice: Red Apple

Bimbo Juice: Veggie

Bimbo Juice Gone Wild: The Muse

Bimbo Juice Gone Wild: Street Racer

Bimbo Juice Gone Wild: Score

Bimbos of the Traveling Earrings: Book 1

Bimbos of the Traveling Earrings: Book 2

Bimbos of the Traveling Earrings: Book 3

Bimbos of the Traveling Earrings: Book 4

Bimbo Party: Kennedy

Bimbo Party: Esme

Bimbo Party: Ariana

Bimbo Party: Tara

Workout Buddies

Wishful Thinking

Wanting More

Bimbo Harem: Annabelle

Bimbo Harem: Josie

Bimbo Harem: Nikki

Bimbo Harem: Tiana

Giggle Dust

Giggle Dust 2.0

Giggle Dust 3.0

Giggle Dust 4.0

Bimbo Takeover: The First Step

Bimbo Takeover: Teammates

Bimbo Takeover: Going to the Top

Bimbo Takeover: Revenge of the Bimbos

Thanks for the Mammaries

A New Beginning

Copying Kat

Spreading the Love

Discovering Eden

Building Eden

Spring In Eden

Saving Eden

The Perfect Girlfriend

The Perfect Engagement

The Perfect Wife

The Perfect Woman

Be Hot, Not Smart

No Thoughts for Thots

Be Art, Not Smart

Forbidden Obsession

Goddess Within

The Message

Bimbo Queen

Bachelorette

Beneath the Gown

Honeymoon Surprise

New Rules

Embrace It

Not So Smart

Best of Friends

Joining Bimbodom

Bimbo Salon

Bimbo Vision

Spiral

Rerun

www.ingramcontent.com/pod-product-compliance
Lightning Source LLC
Chambersburg PA
CBHW031242130726
47988CB00008B/3204